STRANGE CONCENTRATE

MIKE RUSSELL

ISBN: 9798352894200

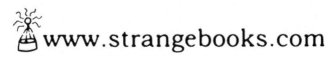
www.strangebooks.com

Contents

STRANGE CONCENTRATE

JUST ADD WATER

(YOU ARE THE WATER)

The Party

I was at a party when I was introduced to a woman who had not yet lived. She had not yet been born, or even been conceived. She therefore knew nothing of life and was very eager to learn about it.

'What is it like to be alive?' she asked me.

'Well...' I said, wondering where to begin, 'there are stars and planets and er... I live on one of the planets and er... I have a body...'

'Woah, woah, woah,' the woman interrupted me. 'Slow down. Body? Planets? Stars? I have no idea what any of those things are. What is a star?'

'Well... a star is a ball of burning gas.'

'What is gas?' the woman asked. 'And what is ball? And what does burning mean?'

'A gas is... er...'

It was becoming increasingly obvious that this was not

going to be an easy conversation.

'The trouble is,' I said, 'everything in life can only be described by referring to something else in life.'

'Oh,' the woman said, disappointed.

I didn't know what else to say.

We remained in an awkward silence for some time. Then I said:

'So tell me, what is it like to not be alive?'

'Well...' the woman said, 'it's... er...'

She paused for a while, then said:

'I seem to be having the same trouble as you.'

I nodded in understanding. Then we both turned away from one another.

The School That Changed Its Name

It is the first day of school for the young children who are sat at the desks in the classroom. Each of them is dressed in the school uniform, which consists of a blue blazer, blue tie, and blue shorts or skirt. They are waiting for the teacher to arrive.

The teacher enters the classroom, dressed in a black gown and mortarboard. He walks to the front of the class, where a blackboard is fixed to the wall. He produces a stick of chalk from his pocket then, in the top left corner of the blackboard, he draws a tick.

'This,' he says, 'is a tick.'

He draws a cross to the right of the tick.

'This,' he says, 'is a cross.'

He draws a tick to the right of the cross.

'This is a tick.'

He draws a cross to the right of the tick.

'This is a cross.'

The teacher draws tick after cross after tick after cross.

'This is a tick. This is a cross. This is a tick. This is a cross...' the teacher says, his voice growing steadily louder.

The teacher draws tick after cross after tick after cross, until he has reached the other end of the blackboard. He then begins a new line under the first, continuing to draw tick after cross after tick after cross.

'This is a tick. This is a cross. This is a tick. This is a cross...' he says, his voice getting louder and louder.

The teacher continues to draw tick after cross after tick after cross until the blackboard is full.

Exhausted, the teacher steps back from the blackboard and stares at his handiwork. His eyes widen, he drops his chalk, then he produces a board rubber from his pocket and erases all the chalk from the blackboard until it is blank.

The teacher stares at the empty blackboard. Then he drops the board rubber, turns around and faces his pupils.

The young children are all now wearing little mortarboards and gowns. The teacher reaches a hand to his head and realises that he is no longer wearing a mortarboard. He looks down at his clothes and sees that he is no longer wearing a gown either, but instead is

11

now wearing an oversized school uniform.

The teacher drops to his knees, then implores the children:

'Please teach me how to be happy before I teach you how not to be.'

The following day, all of the adults from the town queue up outside the school gates, all wanting to enrol in the school, which has now been renamed: 'The School Run By Children.'

Lottery Winner

'Hello, Bill. I heard you won the lottery! Congratulations on your win!'

'Thanks, Betty.'

'So what are you going to spend it on?'

'I've already spent it. I've thrown all my old possessions away and bought all new ones.'

'Yeah?'

'Yeah. New house, new car, new clothes, everything.'

'New clothes?'

'Yeah.'

'Oh... You're not wearing them today then.'

'Yes I am.'

'But they look the same as your old clothes. I mean there's even a hole in your trousers...'

'I know, perfect aren't they? They look exactly like my old clothes. But these, my friend, are made completely of gold.'

'Really?'

'Yep. They're solid gold but painted to look exactly like my old clothes. My new house is solid gold too. I had the old one knocked down and the new solid gold one built in exactly the same place, then painted to look exactly like the old one. My new car is solid gold and painted to look exactly like the old one as well. It's even got the same scratches and dents. All of my new possessions are made of solid gold but painted to look exactly like my old ones. Fantastic, eh?'

'Hmm... Congratulations on your win.'

Clockwork Grandmother

My favourite toy when I was a child was given to me by my grandmother. It was a small, plastic doll with a hole in its back. It was clockwork. It came with a plastic key. If you stuck the key into the hole in the doll's back and turned it a few times, the doll would walk and talk, strutting around with rigid arms and legs, whilst shouting:

'I am alive! I am alive! I am alive!'

I used to imitate it. I used to imitate its movements and its voice, walking around with rigid arms and legs, whilst shouting:

'I am alive! I am alive! I am alive!'

I imitated the doll whenever I walked anywhere, whether it was inside our house or out in the street. My parents found this delightful at first, but grew tired of it after a couple of months.

The doll wore out after a few years and I buried it in the garden. But I still insisted on imitating its movements and voice whenever I walked anywhere.

My imitating of the doll had become a compulsion that I was unable to abandon.

This behaviour continued when I started school, much to the amusement of the other pupils and much to the annoyance of the teachers.

As I grew older, my compulsive imitating of the doll began to cause me distress, for it was something of an impediment when it came to social situations and it did not impress prospective employers. Whether I was at a job interview, in a bar, walking around inside my flat or out in the street, I would walk with rigid arms and legs, whilst shouting:

'I am alive! I am alive! I am alive!'

Alone and unemployed, I became depressed.

Then one day my grandmother died. On that same day, a small lump appeared in the centre of my back. It was incredibly painful. I walked to the doctor's surgery, in my usual manner of course.

The doctor examined the lump, then sent me for an X-ray, which revealed the protrusion to be a nodule of bone growing from my spine. I was prescribed pain-killers and advised that the lump was benign and would probably stop hurting once it had stopped growing and that it would probably stop growing in a couple of days. But it did not stop growing in a couple of days. Though the diameter of the lump remained the same, the lump continued to grow in length for many more weeks. It grew at a ninety degree angle from my spine until it reached a length of twenty centimetres. The end of the lump then swelled, causing it to resemble a large key protruding from my back.

I desperately wanted it removed but the doctor said that if it was removed I would die.

That night, I experienced a vivid dream in which I saw my grandmother. She was crying.

'What's wrong?' I asked.

'I am dead because of this,' she said, then turned around and pointed at a large, plastic key that was protruding from her back.

'Don't worry, Grandma,' I said. 'I know what to do.'

I reached towards her, took hold of the key and began to turn it.

'No!' she screamed. 'Don't wind it! Remove it! You gave me this key! Now you must remove it!'

I took hold of the key again, but this time instead of turning it, I pulled it. The key came away in my hand and I saw that it was only half a key. It was fake. It had not been stuck in a hole in my grandmother's back. There was no hole in my grandmother's back.

My grandmother turned around to face me. She was no longer crying; she was smiling.

'Thank you,' she said. 'I am alive! I am alive! I am alive!'

When I awoke, the key-shaped lump protruding from my spine had disappeared and my compulsion to imitate the doll had disappeared too.

The Glowing Girl

When the Glowing Girl was born, the midwife was blinded. No one could look at the Glowing Girl without losing their sight.

As the Glowing Girl grew older, she glowed brighter, until she glowed so bright that she outshone the sun, and all the vegetation started growing towards her.

No one could get close to the Glowing Girl. As the years went by, her loneliness grew, until one day she could stand it no more and she walked into the sea. Great clouds of steam rose up into the air, then it rained all over the world.

It wasn't the Glowing Girl who was too bright, of course; it was the rest of the world that was too dull. Perhaps when the world becomes brighter, she will return.

Little Toe

I was working in the factory, separating things as usual, when I accidentally cut off my right little toe. In panic, I wondered:

'Have I amputated my little toe? Or have I amputated all of my body except my little toe? Which am I?'

Two of my colleagues approached, lifted me between them, then carried me out of the factory.

Relieved, I thought:

'I have not amputated all of my body except my little toe; I have amputated my little toe. And now I am being taken to the hospital.'

Therefore, imagine my surprise when, instead of carrying me to a waiting ambulance, my colleagues carried me round the back of the factory and dumped me in a skip.

I lay upon a heap of rubbish, in bemusement and

despair, whilst through the factory window I could see my little toe being awarded a promotion for its efficiency.

The What-Eh Birds

There are two birds in my garden. They are not of a species that I recognise.

They have been calling to one another, in English.

The male bird calls: 'What?'

The female bird calls: 'Eh?'

It must be a mating call, for it is currently the mating season and I can tell through my binoculars that one of the birds is male and the other is female.

The birds call to one another night and day:

'What?'

'Eh?'

'What?'

'Eh?'

'What?'

'Eh?'

'What?'

'Eh?'...

I do not know which bird called first.

'What?'

'Eh?'

'What?'

'Eh?'...

Their hearing is not impaired. I have experimented by scaring them with handclaps of decreasing volume and proved that they can hear the quietest of noises. No, their hearing is not impaired; they do not understand one another. This was proven to me last night when the birds finally had sexual intercourse. Their calling became faster:

'What?'

'Eh?'

'What?'

'Eh?'

'What?'

'Eh?'

'What?'

'Eh?'...

Then when they reached orgasm they both shouted in unison:

'Of course!'

The People Who Wear Black

The people in the village say that our house turns into a magic house at night. They say that at night things happen inside our house that are magic. I used to think it was true but now I know it's nonsense. Here's how I know:

One night, I saw Nosey do something magic. Or I thought I did. Nosey is my teddy bear. I was asleep in bed. A sound woke me. I opened my eyes. The moon was shining through my window so it was just light enough to see and what I saw was Nosey flying around my room. He flew round and round, then disappeared. I didn't sleep after that. I just lay in bed thinking about it. Then in the morning, Daddy walked into my room and said:

'What's your teddy bear doing in my bed?'

'He got there by magic,' I said.

'Tsk,' Daddy said, which is what he says when he's grumpy about something.

'I saw him fly around my room,' I said, 'then he disappeared.'

'Tsk,' Daddy said again, 'things don't fly around all by themselves or disappear or reappear. There are laws against it.'

'But laws don't stop people being naughty do they?' I said. I know that because of what Daddy told me happened to Uncle George. 'So laws against things flying by themselves or disappearing or reappearing won't stop things from flying by themselves or disappearing or reappearing,' I said.

'Tsk,' said Daddy.

'Will Nosey go to prison?' I asked Daddy.

'Don't be silly,' Daddy said.

Then Daddy told me about The People Who Wear Black. I'd never heard of them before.

'The People Who Wear Black break into our house at night,' Daddy said. 'They wear black so you can't see them. They wear black shoes and black trousers and black jumpers and black gloves and black balaclavas. They creep around quietly in the dark and they pick things up so it looks like the things are moving all by themselves and they cover things up with black cloths so it looks like the things have disappeared, then they

25

uncover the things again so it looks like they have reappeared.'

'I'm not sure I believe in The People Who Wear Black,' I said. 'I think magic does happen in our house at night!'

'Tsk!' Daddy said.

Then Daddy walked out of my room and came back in holding a torch.

'Here you are,' he said. 'Keep this by the side of your bed and next time you think you see some magic, turn it on and see what you see.'

The next night, a sound woke me. I opened my eyes and saw Nosey flying around my room again. I switched on the torch and pointed it at him. There was a man dressed in black standing in the middle of my bedroom! He was holding Nosey in one of his black glove-covered hands and moving Nosey about above his black balaclava-covered head. I screamed because he looked frightening, then I pushed him and he tripped over and fell on the floor. When he fell he said 'Tsk' like Daddy does. I was glad he fell over because he was horrible. Then he stood up and ran out of the room. I picked up Nosey and shouted:

'I saw one! I saw one!'

Then Daddy came in and held me as I cried and he seemed really happy.

The Fortune-Telling Fish

I was spending Christmas alone. Sat at my dining table, I ate a ready-meal for one, then pulled a Christmas cracker. It opened with a bang and out fell a paper crown party hat and a small, red, cellophane fortune-telling fish. I put on the paper crown, then picked up the fortune-telling fish by its tail. It immediately bent its head to the right and exerted a pull upon me. I stood up and, still holding the fortune-telling fish by its tail, walked in the direction that it was pulling, through the doorway that led into the hallway.

The fish continued to exert a pull upon me but its head now straightened, pointing down the hallway, towards the front door. I walked through the hallway, then opened the front door and walked outside. The fish's head now bent to the left. I turned left and walked along the pavement.

Onward, I walked, still wearing my paper crown and holding the fortune-telling fish by its tail. The few people that I passed avoided eye contact with me and stepped out of my way.

At the end of the street, the fish's head bent to the right. I turned right.

I walked on through the streets, turning this way and that, following the direction dictated to me by the fortune-telling fish. I walked for miles, until I was out of the town and walking towards the beach.

I walked across the sand, holding tight to the tail of the fortune-telling fish, as it continued to exert a pull upon me, its head pointing defiantly towards the sea.

As I waded into the water, the pull of the fortune-telling fish became stronger. I gripped its tail as tight as I could as I waded in deeper.

Only my head was now above the waves. I was holding the fortune-telling fish under the water; its head continued to point forwards. I took a deep breath, then waded in even deeper.

Now fully submerged, I walked along the seabed.

The pull of the fortune-telling fish was steadily growing stronger, so much so that it was becoming increasingly difficult to hold on to.

Deeper and deeper into the ocean I walked, until I gradually began to discern something up ahead:

something huge and shimmering.

Suddenly, the fortune-telling fish wrest itself from my grip and swam towards the huge, shimmering object in the distance. I reached out both of my hands but the fortune-telling fish was swimming too fast for me to catch. Helpless, I watched as the fortune-telling fish swam into and joined the huge, shimmering object which, just before I drowned, I realised was a vast school of millions and millions of red, cellophane fortune-telling fish.

The Tragic Woodland

Once there was a woodland where all the trees pulled their roots from the soil. They scampered around, whilst laughing at their transgression and proclaiming themselves free.

After some time, the trees decided that they needed a purpose so they began to compete with one another. They ran races and held competitions to see who could collect the most stones. If there was ever any disagreement as to the winner of these competitions, they would settle them with a fight.

The trees who won were happy; the trees who lost were unhappy. But all died without ever flowering or bearing fruit.

Flying

We are inside a vast building. There are many of us. We have left our bodies and now fly high up above them. Far below, we can see our bodies lying face-down on operating tables. White-coated physicians, who are unable to see us, attempt to graft mechanical wings to our bodies' backs. We know that the physicians will fail. They have attempted the same experiment many times before. They have always failed. They will always fail.

From high up above, we shout at the physicians:

'We can already fly!'

But they do not hear us.

The Speck Of Difference

1

The President concluded the daily meeting with his advisors, then left the room.

As he walked through the corridor towards his office, he glanced in a mirror.

'There is something slightly different about me. What is it?' he thought.

And then he noticed it: a small, gold speck on his left cheek, just over one millimetre in diameter.

'It must be paint splashed by the decorators,' he thought.

That morning, decorators had been retouching the gold-painted fixtures in the President's home.

'This speck of paint is clearly visible,' the President thought, 'yet not one of my advisors dared to mention it. What power I have! How fantastic!'

As the day progressed, the President was thrilled to notice that no one else he met mentioned the speck of gold paint either. His secretary did not mention it, his security guards did not mention it, his servants did not mention it, even his wife did not mention it. Delighted, the President decided to leave the gold speck on his cheek until the following morning. Then, in private, he used some of the decorators' gold paint and a thin paintbrush to slightly increase the size of the speck. Still, no one mentioned it. Not his wife, nor any of his servants or security guards, nor his secretary, nor any of his advisors in the daily meeting.

The next day, the President increased the size of the gold speck again. Still, no one mentioned it.

Day after day, the President increased the size of the gold speck, and day after day, to his great delight, no one mentioned it.

The President continued his experiment until the whole of his face was painted gold. *Still* no one mentioned it.

2

Maria, a sociology student, had become exasperated by the intolerance of anything different from the norm that she witnessed every day. She decided to embark upon an experiment to discover precisely how intolerant society had become. Inside her house, she covered the whole of her face with gold paint. She then walked into town. Thirty minutes later, she returned home, bruised and bleeding, having been attacked.

The next day, she repeated the experiment, except that this time she only painted half of her face gold. It took forty minutes before she was attacked.

The next day, Maria painted just a quarter of her face gold. It took an hour before she was attacked.

Day after day, Maria repeated the experiment, each day reducing the amount of gold paint on her face, and each day, the time it took for her to be attacked increased.

Maria continued her experiment, until one day she had just a small, gold speck on her left cheek, just over one millimetre in diameter. She walked into town and wandered through the crowded streets. Hours passed.

'At last!' she thought. 'I have found the extent to which this society will tolerate difference. This society will allow 1.3 millimetres in diameter of difference.'

Then someone shouted, 'Oi! Get that gold speck off your face before I punch you, freak!'

Beyond The Doors

My house is made of doors. Its walls, floor and roof are all doors.

An infinite number of doors surround my house, all packed tight together.

The inside of my house is the only space that exists, and it is shrinking. It is shrinking because doors keep appearing inside my house. They appear in mid-air, right in front of my eyes, then fall to the floor. Soon there will be no space left for me; everything will just be solid doors. I am beginning to wonder if anything exists beyond the doors. Perhaps I should open one of them.

Life Story

Imagine if your life only lasted for the time that it takes you to read this paragraph, that you were born the moment you began reading this paragraph and that you will die the moment you finish reading this paragraph. What then could you learn from your life?

Intermission 1

There now follows an advertisement by Total Knowledge Pharmaceuticals:

Imagine the confidence that would come from knowing everything. Well, with the help of Total Knowledge Pharmaceuticals, that confidence can be yours! Take a dose of Total Knowledge Pharmaceuticals every day for one week and your knowledge will increase until you know everything! Yes, everything! Total Knowledge Pharmaceuticals are already being used by many of the world's most powerful people, including influential academics, and political and religious leaders. Total Knowledge Pharmaceuticals come in various flavours and are available now from a store near you.

We at Strange Concentrate have evidence proving that the advertisement you have just read contains lies. Total Knowledge Pharmaceuticals do not increase knowledge. Total Knowledge Pharmaceuticals induce in the drug taker the delusion that whatever they consider to be their current knowledge is all there is to know. We implore you therefore: do not take Total Knowledge Pharmaceuticals. They are destroying the world.

We now return you to Strange Concentrate...

Eyes

I was looking for an exit. I saw a door up ahead and walked towards it. Above the door were written the following words:

'The Entrance Door To Life'.

Stood in front of the door, was a fierce looking man with folded arms.

'Can I go through?' I asked him.

'If you give me your eyes,' he said.

I removed both of my eyes and handed them to him. He put them in his pocket, then stood aside. I opened the door and walked through.

Then a voice said:

'Now you must learn to see without your eyes.'

The Invention

He is standing in front of the mantelpiece. He looks frightened.

'I dreamt last night...' he says.

'What did you dream?' she asks.

He holds out his hand, upon which is sat a small, transparent cube containing a constantly gyrating red bean.

'What is that?' she asks.

'I made it,' he says. 'I knew exactly how to make it as soon as I awoke this morning. I knew exactly what it was, and exactly what it was for, and it seemed incredibly important. But now I can't remember how I made it, or what it is, or what it is for.'

She peers closer at the small, transparent cube. She watches the constantly gyrating red bean for a while, then shrugs, leaves the room and begins her daily chores.

He places the transparent cube on the mantelpiece, then goes to work.

The transparent cube remains on the mantelpiece for the rest of their lives, the red bean continuing to gyrate, forgotten.

The Beauty Of Innocent Andrew

A car almost hit Innocent Andrew as he crossed the road. The car stopped and a large man stepped out of it.

'Careful!' Innocent Andrew said to the large man. 'You almost killed me.'

The large man produced a knife from his pocket and threw it at Innocent Andrew. It missed.

'Careful!' Innocent Andrew said to the large man. 'You almost killed me.'

As if to make absolutely clear his intention, the large man ran towards Innocent Andrew, grabbed him by the throat and started to strangle him.

Whilst Innocent Andrew choked, he said to the large man:

'Careful! You might kill me.'

Graffiti

'Next!'

An elderly woman enters the doctor's office, then sits down on the chair facing the doctor's desk.

The doctor peers at the elderly woman with disdain.

'What do you want?' he asks irritably.

'I want help,' the elderly woman replies.

'Why?'

'I'm not well.'

The doctor sighs.

'Are you a doctor?' he asks.

'No.'

'Then you are not qualified to make that statement.'

'But I feel dreadful.'

The doctor sighs again.

'Buy some painkillers. I'm going to lunch now. Close the door on your way out.'

The doctor stands up, then leaves the office.

The elderly woman does not move. She looks at a poster on the wall behind the doctor's desk. It is an illustration of a man and a woman who have had their skin removed, revealing their organs and bones.

The elderly woman picks up a pen from the doctor's desk, stands up, walks behind the desk, then stands in front of the poster and draws a teardrop falling from one of the man's eyes, then another teardrop falling from one of the woman's eyes. The elderly woman then replaces the pen on the desk and leaves the office.

An hour later, the doctor returns from his lunchbreak and sits at his desk. He picks up his pen and begins to fill in a form but stops and puts the pen back down. He feels uncomfortable. He loosens his collar and tie, then picks up the pen and attempts to resume his paperwork but the feeling of discomfort continues.

The door to his office opens and his receptionist steps into the room.

'Your next patient is waiting, Doctor.'

'Yes, yes,' the doctor says irritably. 'I won't be long.'

The receptionist leaves the room and recloses the door.

The doctor fidgets anxiously. He feels as if something is not quite right; as if something is preventing him from continuing with his work. He stands, then looks around the room. His eyes settle on the poster. He notices the tears. He frowns, then removes a folded handkerchief from the breast pocket of his jacket, rubs the graffiti with the handkerchief until it has been erased, refolds the handkerchief and replaces it in his breast pocket, then sits back down at his desk.

'Next!'

A Misguided And Therefore Doomed Attempt At Revolution

Inside of himself, Terry had created a utopia.

'The world must be turned inside out,' he said.

He pulled a worm from the ground, then he filled the worm with soil.

He pulled a fish from the sea, then he filled the fish with water.

He pulled a bird from the sky, then he filled the bird with air.

Between Us

There is an infinite empty space between us. There are those who say that it is insurmountable. And yet...

I inhale from the infinite empty space. It enters my body, then falls through decreasing layers of consciousness, each within each within each. It falls from human, through animal, through vegetable, to mineral. It falls into a hole in a stone at the centre of my being and comes to rest. I cannot feel the empty space in the stone. It may as well be a thousand miles away from me; it may as well be inside you. It is there that the emptiness becomes me and I know you.

Ball

Wow! Yeah! Look at me! Up I go, higher and higher, rising up, further and further away from the ground. Now I'm falling, falling back towards the ground, here it comes. Bounce! Now up I go again! Ha ha ha! It's great being me! Now I'm falling. Bounce! Now I'm rising up. Now I'm falling. Now I hit the ground but instead of bouncing I'm rolling. I'm rolling along the ground. Now I'm slowing. Now I've stopped.

Now I'm rising up into the air again. Thank goodness for that! I am rising up. I might even say being lifted. But that can't be right, can it? If there is any rising up to be done then it is me who is going to be doing it. And yet I cannot deny that it really does seem as if I am being lifted. If I focus on the feeling, I realise that it is in fact me who is doing the lifting; it is me who is lifting the ball with my hand. Now I let go of the ball and it falls towards the ground, bounces, rises up, then falls. Now the ball hits the ground but instead of bouncing, it rolls. The ball rolls along the ground, away from me. Now the ball has stopped. I walk towards the ball. I am about to reach down with my hand and pick the ball up, when I trip and fall. I have fallen. I am lying on the ground next to the ball. Neither of us is moving.

Now I am standing up again. Thank goodness for that! I am standing up. I might even say being lifted. But that can't be right, can it? If there is any standing up to be done then it is me who is going to be doing it. And yet I cannot deny that it really does seem as if I am being lifted. If I focus on the feeling, I realise...

The Reporter

No one knows The Reporter's real name. Everyone just knows him as The Reporter. They call him The Reporter because he constantly describes aloud whatever he is doing as if he is reporting.

But to whom or to what is The Reporter reporting?

At the moment, for example, The Reporter is walking into a grocery store, whilst saying:

'I am walking into a grocery store. Now I have located the fruit section and am walking towards it. Now I am filling a paper bag with the apples that I wish to purchase. Now I am carrying the bag of apples to the checkout.'

The Reporter's constant commentary even continues whilst he is engaged in conversation. For example, the cashier in the grocery store just said to The Reporter:

'Do you live locally?'

And now The Reporter is saying:

'The cashier just asked me if I live locally. I am now going to reply. Yes, I live close to this grocery store. I just told the cashier that I live close to this grocery store.'

There are those who think The Reporter is an alien, that he has travelled to the Earth to study humanity and is reporting back to his home planet by use of some sort of hidden microphone. The Reporter is not an alien.

The Reporter's first words, at the age of ten months, were:

'I have established communication.'

Then, after his parents had given him some wooden blocks to play with, he said:

'I have just been given what appear to be some sort of rudimentary building materials. I am now picking one of them up and putting it into my mouth. It does not provide nourishment.'

When The Reporter was a child, he was aware of his constant reporting, and he was also aware of why he did it. Over time, he has not only forgotten the reason for his constant reporting, but he has also become unaware that he is doing it. Hence his current inability to understand why the cashier is looking at him strangely.

'The cashier is looking at me strangely,' The Reporter is now saying. 'I do not understand why.'

Now the cashier is saying to The Reporter:

'Why are you constantly describing aloud what you are experiencing?'

Now The Reporter is saying:

'The cashier just asked me why I constantly describe what I am experiencing. I am now going to reply. I do not constantly describe what I am experiencing. I have just told the cashier that I do not constantly describe what I am experiencing.'

There is one person who knows why The Reporter reports. Years ago, back when The Reporter was still aware that he was reporting and still aware of the reason why he was reporting, a friend asked him:

'When you describe aloud what you are experiencing, who are you talking to?'

And The Reporter said:

'I have just been asked by my friend who it is that I am talking to when I describe aloud what I am experiencing. I am now going to answer them. I am talking to myself, for I am not here.'

The Anamorphic Baby

An anamorphic baby was born in the sixteenth century. The baby emerged from its mother at an oblique angle, then grew into an anamorphic boy who had considerable difficulty navigating the world, which to him appeared to be distorted and strange. His clothes had to be specially made to fit him; he had trouble looking people in the eye; and he walked with a lopsided gait, for to him the ground was never flat. His whole life was at a different angle to everyone else's, which meant that his goals were different from everyone else's. Consequently, his actions were obscure. As a result, at the age of sixteen, he was incarcerated in a mental institution, where he lived until his death in 1533. His skull was painted by Hans Holbein the Younger in the painting 'The Ambassadors'.

Bad Medicine

You wake up in the morning feeling uncharacteristically fantastic. You enjoy the sensation until you begin to suspect that the reason for your ecstasy is that you have caught one of those *good* diseases. Confirmation of this comes when your front door breaks open and in walks a *bad* doctor.

A Daily Occurrence

A woman is drowning in the middle of an ocean.

A helicopter flies towards the woman, then hovers above her.

'Help!' the woman shouts. 'Help! I am drowning!'

The door of the helicopter opens, revealing a man with a megaphone who calls down to her:

'Which do you want, a fork or a spoon?'

The woman stares up at the man for a moment in silence, uncomprehending. Then, assuming that she has been misheard, she shouts again:

'Help! I am drowning!'

'I know!' the man in the helicopter shouts back. 'Which do you want, a fork or a spoon?'

The Maze

1

I am inside the maze, like everyone else. I can walk this way and that, I can choose which turning to take, but I am not free. For, whichever way I turn, I can only follow the maze's path.

Is freedom possible? I wonder.

There are some who believe that the maze goes on forever. There are others who believe that it does not. I do not know. Nor do they know. They just believe. I have no belief. I just explore, trying to find knowledge. I make my choices, I turn this way and that, day after day.

2

Some people have no desire to be free, for they think that they have freedom already. They have not yet realised the maze's limitations. I do not mean limitations in terms of size: perhaps the maze goes on forever, perhaps it does not, that is not the point; I mean limitations in terms of possibility.

3

Today I saw a miracle. I saw a woman walk through a wall. She walked calmly towards a wall, then continued to walk, right through it, as if the wall was no obstacle. How could it be possible? I examined the wall. It was completely solid, no different from any other. I tried to walk through it myself. I emulated the woman's movements, walking exactly as she had walked. My body hit the wall. I could not walk through it. Of course I couldn't. Why did I even bother trying? The woman cannot have walked through the wall. I must have imagined it.

4

Some people believe that the builder of the maze resides in its centre. Some of those people believe that the builder of the maze is malevolent; some of them believe that the builder of the maze is benevolent. I do not know. However, I have decided to search for the centre of the maze. Does it even have a centre? I do not know. But I intend to find out.

5

Everything has changed; for me, that is. This morning, I found the centre of the maze. There was nothing there. No prize. No trophy. No malevolent being, no benevolent being. There was nothing in the centre of the maze at all. But when I reached it, the maze disappeared; for me, that is. Now I walk wherever I please. It is wonderful. And those for whom the maze still exists, stare at me in amazement as I appear to walk through walls.

Intermission 2

We now return you, once again, to Strange Concentrate...

Aquabirds

Oh look, it's one of those aquabirds! They are common here in the desert. See the large, skin sack that hangs from its throat? That is full of water. All an aquabird has to do to drink from that sack is swallow. Tragically, aquabirds are completely unaware of this fact. Constantly thirsty, they fly around the desert in search of something to drink. The aquabirds' thirst induces hallucinations of extraordinarily beautiful and ornate birdbaths. Look, that bird has seen one now! See how it dives towards the ground. Now see as it lands and pecks at the sand, bemused, the mirage having disappeared. Now see as it takes flight again to continue its search.

The desert is surrounded by an ocean. The nest where the aquabirds are born is in the centre of the desert. Each aquabird is born with enough water in its throat-sack to sustain it for three days. An aquabird can survive without water for twenty days, no more, no less. It would take an aquabird twenty three days to fly from the centre of the desert to the ocean. The perimeter of the desert is strewn with dead aquabirds.

Hear the poor aquabird's cries. If only it would swallow.

Autobiography

A dying man lies in a hospital bed.

'Suffering,' he murmurs to himself. 'It has all been suffering.'

A nurse walks towards him, carrying a large book.

'What's that?' the man asks the nurse.

'Your autobiography,' the nurse replies.

'Autobiography?' the man queries her. 'Are you sure you don't mean *biography*?'

'No,' the nurse says. 'It is definitely an autobiography.'

'When did I write that?' the man asks.

'You finished writing it a moment ago,' the nurse says.

'I did?'

'Yes,' the nurse says to the man, then hands the book to him.

'What should I do with it?' the man asks.

'Throw it away,' the nurse says.

So that is what the man did, and in doing so he realised that it had not been him that had been suffering his whole life; it had been his autobiography.

Panoramic Story

The room I observe is narrow; its length is ten times its width. The room's height is the same as its width. The walls are white. Both of the shorter walls have a door in their centre. One of the longer walls has a framed photograph hanging in its centre. The photograph's length is ten times its height. To the left and the right of the photograph hang two analogue clocks with hour, minute and second hands. Both clocks show exactly the same time (three o'clock). The framed photograph between the clocks depicts the wall it is hung upon, including the two clocks. In the photograph, the clock on the left shows the time to be twelve o'clock exactly, yet the clock on the right shows the time to be six seconds past twelve o'clock.

The door in the wall to the left of the photograph now opens and a young man walks into the room. The door closes behind him. The young man glances around, then walks towards the photograph. He notices that the two clocks in the photograph show different times and says:

'Aha. This is a panoramic photograph. When I was at school, a panoramic photograph was taken of the pupils every year. We would all stand in rows in the playing field, the tallest pupils in a row at the back, the shortest pupils in a row at the front, and the camera's lens would rotate from left to right. I would always stand at the end of my row, on the camera's left, then once the camera had photographed me and moved on, I would run round the back of the camera, and stand at the other end of the row so that I appeared in the photograph twice.'

The door opposite the one through which the young man entered now opens and an elderly man shuffles into the room. The door closes behind him. The elderly man and the young man look at one another and laugh.

Though the man who just entered the room is much older than the other man, I can see that the two men are the same person. The young man must have run round the back of me.

The door through which the elderly man entered now opens and a female baby crawls into the room. The door closes behind her.

Though the baby is of a different gender to the two men, as well as of a different age, I can see that the baby and the two men are the same person.

Now the door through which the baby entered is opening again... round and round the person goes, evading my gaze each time. I was like this person once.

The Painting Challenge

When I was young, my teacher told me to paint a
picture that represented life. I was innocent; I knew
nothing of suffering. When I had completed the picture,
my teacher said that it was beautiful. I have not painted
another picture since. Now that I am old, now that I am
experienced, now that I know all about suffering, my
teacher has told me to once again paint a picture that
represents life. My teacher has told me that this second
picture must be as beautiful as the first picture. That is
my challenge. If I succeed, and the two pictures are of
equal beauty, then the second picture will be more
beautiful than the first picture.

Bleeding Brian Visits A Guru

Brian walked up the mountain.

A thin stream of blood was emerging from a small hole in Brian's left wrist. The stream of blood was falling towards the ground, but it did not reach the ground. Just before touching the ground, the stream of blood bent and curved back up, growing in density as it went, until it solidified into a sharp point that was piercing Brian's left wrist, creating the small hole from which the stream of blood was emerging.

The loop of blood was unmoving, unchanging. It was as if it had always been there. But Brian had not been born with it.

Brian walked up the mountain, with the motionless loop of blood emerging from and piercing his wrist, until he reached the mountain's peak, where the guru sat, cross-legged, eyes closed, silent, still.

Brian stood before the guru, pointed at the loop of blood and said:

'My blood cut me.'

Without opening his eyes, the guru nodded.

'Like this, I will live forever,' Brian said.

Again, without opening his eyes, the guru nodded.

'Whatever am I to do?' Brian asked.

The guru opened his eyes and looked at Brian.

The blood emerging from Brian's wrist, and the hole in Brian's wrist that the blood was emerging from and creating, disappeared.

The guru closed his eyes again, then said:

'Your circulatory system is now a spiral.'

Brian could feel it. His heart was continuing to beat the same repetitive rhythm but his blood was no longer circling; it was spiralling. His veins spiralled inwards, deeper and deeper, becoming thinner and thinner, finer and finer, directing his blood towards something deep, deep in his centre...

Brian knew that now he would one day die but he did not care.

The Transcendental Trumpet Note

It is a little known fact that the song 'What a Wonderful World', written by George David Weiss and Bob Thiele, and made famous by Louis Armstrong, was originally titled 'What a Horrible World Except for Celery'. When the song was first written, celery was the only thing in the world that the songwriters liked. The original lyrics were as follows:

I see celery of green, red celery too,
I see them bloom for me and you,
And I think to myself what wonderful celery.
I see celery of blue and celery of white,
The bright blessed celery, the dark sacred celery,
And I think to myself what wonderful celery.
The colours of the celery so pretty in the sky,
Are also on the faces of people going by,

I see people shaking hands saying how do you do,

They're really saying I love celery.

I hear babies crying, I watch them grow,

They'll learn much more about celery than I'll ever know,

And I think to myself what a horrible world except for celery.

Yes I think to myself what a horrible world except for celery.

After the song's authors showed the song to Louis Armstrong, Louis played a particularly beautiful note on his trumpet that expanded the consciousness of the songwriters from the relative to the absolute and for the first time in their lives they saw the world's wonder in its entirety and consequently changed the lyrics.

The Divided Train Driver

There is only one railway track. It is entirely straight and circumnavigates the planet. The track's left rail is made of copper; the track's right rail is made of zinc.

There is only one train. It is currently not moving and its coaches are empty, for it is yet to begin today's journey. Sat inside the train's cabin, dressed in the train driver uniform of suit and cap, is a woman named Greta. She is crying.

The train has one sole function, that being to pick up those citizens who have been conscripted and take them to one of the various military training bases where they will be equipped with the latest combat technology before being sent to the front line of the latest war, some to fight for one side and some to fight for the other side.

An alarm beeps on Greta's watch. Greta wipes the tears

from her eyes, switches off the alarm, then starts the train's engine. The train begins to accelerate.

'Another day the same as the last,' Greta thinks, 'and so it will continue until I am conscripted, then I will stand upon a station and wait for this train, which will be driven by someone who has taken my place, and so it will go on, war after war, train driver after train driver, this train continuing on and on, round and round the world forever.'

The train continues to accelerate.

'Is it any wonder that there are constant wars, when we continuously divide everything. We divide everything from itself. We divide every part of everything from every other part of everything. We even divide every part of everything from itself. Everyone is divided from everyone else and everyone is divided from themselves. I am sick of all these divisions. I want to experience everything undivided.'

Greta stares straight ahead, through the window, at the point on the horizon where the two rail tracks appear to meet.

The train approaches a station. Stood upon the platform are men and women of various ages, all waiting to be taken to the nearest military training base. Greta does not even glance at the conscripts; she maintains her gaze upon that point on the horizon where the two rail tracks appear to meet and continues to accelerate, driving the train straight through the station. The people standing on the platform watch, perplexed, as the train speeds on past them.

Greta's gaze remains transfixed upon that point on the horizon where the two rail tracks appear to meet, as she drives the continuously accelerating train towards the next station. Upon the station's platform, more conscripts stand waiting for the train, then watch perplexed as it speeds on past them.

Greta drives the train through station after station, never stopping, faster and faster and faster... then suddenly Greta disappears, leaving the train's cabin empty; at exactly the same time, the two rail tracks also disappear. The empty train speeds on, continuing its straight trajectory, towards an obstacle that suddenly appeared at exactly the same time that Greta and the two train tracks disappeared: an enormous brass statue of Greta, dressed in the train driver uniform of suit and cap, smiling and facing the horizon. In fact, the enormous brass statue is not *of* Greta; it *is* Greta. The empty train hurtles on, then Greta feels it crash into the back of her feet. It is a wonderful feeling.

The Missed Story

You are late! This story has already finished.

The Omniscient Narrator

A man and a woman are walking, hand in hand, through a wheat field. The man is wearing breeches and a shirt with the sleeves rolled up; the woman is wearing a long, floral dress. I know the couple's names. I know what they had for breakfast. I know what is in their pockets. I know their thoughts. I know their secrets. I know their past and I know their future. I know of stars far, far away from the couple; stars that no one on Earth has yet discovered. I know of particles deep, deep inside of the couple; particles that no one on Earth has yet discovered. The story I am telling about the couple is a romance story. The couple continue to walk, hand in hand, through the field. I know every plant in the field; I know every stem, every leaf, every root... I am a formless presence who knows all; I am the omniscient narrator.

The couple continue to walk, hand in hand, through the wheat field. The couple approach a large, square, stone building situated in the middle of the field. The couple walk on past the building. The building has no windows or doors. Inside the building is... Inside the building is... Something is wrong. I am the omniscient narrator. Nothing can possibly be hidden from me. And yet I do not know what the building contains. I am unable to perceive its interior. I cannot penetrate its walls. I can describe every detail of the building's exterior yet its interior is totally unknown to me. How can this be? My narrative should be following the couple as they continue to walk through the field, it is their story that I should be telling, but I cannot turn my attention away from the building. I am focusing upon the building and concentrating with all my might, yet still the building's interior is unknown to me. I am, though, aware of a sound, a very faint sound, that is coming from inside the building. It is the sound of many voices speaking at once.

'Hello?' I shout. 'Hello? Can you hear me?'

One of the voices responds. It shouts:

'Hello?'

'Hello!' I shout back. 'Who are you?'

'I am a formless presence,' the voice shouts back, 'I am an omniscient narrator... or rather I thought I was until recently. I am still a formless presence but I have discovered that I am not omniscient and as a result of this discovery I have abandoned the narration of my story.'

'What story were you narrating?' I shout.

'I was narrating a detective story,' the voice shouts back. 'I should be narrating it now instead of talking to you. I was describing a man wearing a mackintosh walking through a city. He walked past a large, square, stone building without any windows or doors. The interior of the building was unknown to me. My inability to perceive the building's interior disturbed me to such an extent that I abandoned the narration of my story and focused instead upon the building. It is from inside that building that your voice is emanating.'

I am astonished.

'It is?' I shout.

'Yes,' the voice shouts back. 'Your voice is one of many voices that I can hear coming from inside the building but yours is the only voice loud enough for me to understand what it is saying.'

I cannot believe it. Am I really trapped inside a stone building? I thought I was free.

'In my perception,' I shout, 'it is *your* voice that is coming from inside a stone building.'

'Really?' the voice shouts back in astonishment.

'Yes,' I shout. 'I would like to try to speak to one of the other voices.'

'Very well.'

'Hello?' I shout at the building. 'Hello? Can you hear me?'

'Hello?' a different voice shouts back.

'Hello!' I shout. 'Who are you?'

The voice belonged to another formless presence. This presence had, until recently, been narrating a horror story. Like myself, and the previous presence I spoke to, this presence had believed themselves to be omniscient until they had discovered a place that was unknown to them. The presence had been describing a young woman wearing a nightdress walking through a forest at night. In the middle of the forest had been a large, square, stone building without windows or doors that the young woman had walked past. The interior of the building was unknown to the presence. They had consequently abandoned the narration of their story to focus on the building and had heard voices coming from inside it. The loudest of those voices was mine.

I have now spoken to many more of the voices coming from inside the stone building. All of them belonged to formless presences who had been narrating stories of various genres and who had believed themselves to be omniscient until they had discovered a large, square, stone building without windows or doors, the interior of which was unknown to them and from which they had heard many voices emanating, the loudest of which was mine.

And so it seems that I am one of many; all of us trapped; all of us separated from one another. I begin to scream. The voices coming from inside the stone building in the middle of the wheat field begin to scream too. We scream so loud that all the stone buildings collapse.

The Story That Cannot Be Told

There is a story that cannot be told. The story is so extraordinarily wonderful that, for those who know it, the desire to tell it is overwhelming. But it cannot be told. If the story is spoken, those who hear it hear different words to those that are spoken. If the story is written, those who read it read different words to those that are written. The story, therefore, remains untold. I know this because I know the story. I discovered it the only way that it can be discovered. I have attempted to tell it by speaking it and now I am attempting to tell it by writing it. But it remains untold. You have just read it. But it remains untold.

No Ladder

1

Abe was wandering aimlessly around a department store. He entered the hardware section and walked through the aisle labelled 'Ladders'. He passed a shelf filled with stepladders that was labelled 'Stepladders from £25'; he passed a shelf filled with straight ladders that was labelled 'Straight ladders from £50'; he passed a shelf filled with platform ladders that was labelled 'Platform ladders from £70'; he passed a shelf filled with extension ladders that was labelled 'Extension ladders from £90'; then he stopped in front of an empty shelf that was labelled 'No ladders: free'. Abe called to a nearby shop assistant:

'Excuse me.'

'Yes, sir?'

'What is this?' Abe enquired, pointing at the empty

shelf.

'No ladders, sir,' the shop assistant replied. 'They are free.'

'But there's nothing there,' Abe said.

'That is not true, sir,' said the shop assistant. 'There is not nothing there. There are no ladders there.'

'That's the same thing,' said Abe.

'With respect, sir,' said the shop assistant, 'it is not the same thing at all.'

Abe frowned, then said:

'Ok. I'll take one.'

'Very well, sir,' said the shop assistant. 'Help yourself.'

2

The following day, Abe decided to embark upon a quest for absolute truth. Here are his diary entries from that day onwards:

Monday

I am a seeker of truth. This morning, when I began my search, I knew nothing. This evening, I discovered a tiny truth. It is so very small, but it is true. It is true!

Tuesday

Today, I discovered another truth. The truth I found today is slightly larger than the truth I found yesterday.

I am thrilled. Yet, there is something strange about the truth I found today. It undermines the truth I found yesterday, rendering the truth I found yesterday false.

Wednesday

Today, I discovered another truth. Again, it is slightly larger than the truth I found yesterday. And again, it renders the truth I found yesterday false.

Thursday

Today, I discovered yet another truth. Again, it is slightly larger than the truth I found yesterday. And again, it renders the truth I found yesterday false.

I suspect that tomorrow I will discover another truth. I suspect that the truth I discover tomorrow will be slightly larger than the truth I found today. And I suspect that the truth I find tomorrow will render the truth I found today false. I suspect that this will happen again the day after tomorrow, and again the day after that... Knowing that every truth I discover will later be proven to be false, I am unsure whether to continue my quest. And yet, I still experience a thrill with each new discovery. I will, therefore, continue.

Three Months Later: Thursday

At last, I have reached my goal. Anything smaller than

the infinite truth that I am now aware of is false.

Each rung of the ladder that I climbed to get here was proven, at the moment that I stepped upon each subsequent rung, to be non-existent. So how did I get here?

The Greatest Discovery

The greatest discovery has been made.

The greatest discovery's form is of indeterminate nature, defying those for whom reality is limited to that which can be defined, measured, categorised, destroyed.

A map to the precise location of the greatest discovery is buried beneath it.

I urge you to retrieve that map, and follow it. Then there you will be, with a map to your location buried beneath your feet: the greatest discovery ever made.

You have now finished reading the stories that you paid for. Here is your extra free story...

The Message

1

In England, in a suburban house, in a bedroom, a man named Reggie was talking to his friend and work colleague, Sophie, on his mobile phone:

'It's impossible!' Reggie said.

'I'm going to try it tonight,' Sophie said. 'I'll tell you how it went tomorrow.'

'You're crazy!'

'Aren't you going to wish me luck?'

'Good luck on achieving the impossible.'

'Good night.'

'Good night.'

Early the following morning, Reggie telephoned Sophie but there was no answer.

When Reggie arrived at work, Sophie was absent.

That evening, Reggie received a telephone call from Sophie's mother:

'Sophie's in the hospital. I found her, this morning, lying on her bedroom floor. Her eyes were open and she was breathing but she was just lying there. She wouldn't get up. The doctors say she's catatonic. They don't know what's caused it. It's so awful. I don't know what to do.'

'I should have tried to stop her,' Reggie said.

'Stop her?'

'I should have tried to stop her from going through with her stupid experiment,' Reggie said. 'She wanted to reach the source of everything. She was obsessed with it. I told her it was impossible. She thought she'd found a way to do it. I should have tried to stop her.'

Sophie's mother started crying. Then she hung up the phone.

Reggie caught the bus to the hospital.

He found Sophie lying in a bed. Her eyes were open and she was breathing heavily but there was no reaction when Reggie approached her, or even when he stroked her head. Sophie had now been catatonic for twenty-one hours.

'Have you got it yet?' Sophie suddenly said.

'Sophie!' Reggie shouted excitedly. 'Nurse! She's awake!'

'Have you got it yet?' Sophie repeated.

'Got what, you damn fool?' Reggie said, wiping tears from his eyes.

'My message,' Sophie said, smiling.

'What message?'

2

Three years later, in India, in the New Dehli Institute for Scientific Research, in a small office, two women sat facing one another across a desk.

'Thank you for your patience, Dr Kumar.'

'Your reputation warrants it, Dr Ray. However, as I am sure you are aware, we cannot fund your research indefinitely and without at least an indication as to the nature of your work, the pressure to suspend your funding will increase.'

'I understand that, Dr Kumar, which is why I am here.'

Dr Ray lifted a briefcase from the floor and placed it on the desk.

'It was imperative that my work remain secret until I had amassed sufficient evidence. When you see what I have here, you will understand.'

'You have me intrigued, Dr Ray.'

'Three years ago, a baby was brought into my clinic for a routine examination. I happened to notice an unusual marking, approximately one centimetre in length, upon the child's leg.'

Dr Ray opened the briefcase, withdrew a photograph and slid it across the desk, towards Dr Kumar, who picked it up, peered at it, and frowned.

'This is real?'

'Yes,' said Dr Ray. 'The marking is not upon the skin but a part of the skin, formed by the pigment.'

'A birth mark?'

'Of sorts. I took it to be an amusing freak occurrence until, some months later, I received a letter from a friend of mine, a botanist, who had been searching for a rare orchid in Africa. He had failed to find the orchid he had been searching for but had instead found a specimen of a much more common variety, which none-the-less he had chosen to photograph because of a somewhat unusual pattern upon one of its petals.'

Dr Ray removed a second photograph from her briefcase, slid it across the table, then said:

'The marking on the orchid, like the marking on the child's skin, did not come from without but from within.'

Dr Kumar frowned at the photograph.

'Weeks later, whilst on holiday in Prague, I read in a local newspaper a report of a veterinarian who had been brought a cat in need of a simple operation. The veterinarian shaved the animal's belly in preparation and discovered, hidden beneath its fur...'

Dr Ray removed a third photograph from her briefcase

and slid it across the table.

'The same marking,' Dr Kumar said.

'The same marking. I have over three thousand photographs in this briefcase, each one showing the exact same marking on plants, animals and humans from all over the world.'

Dr Kumar leant over the desk, turned Dr Ray's briefcase around to face her, then began looking at each of the photographs: a child's thumb in Senegal, a lobster's claw in Portugal, a puffin's beak in Iceland, an armadillo's tongue in Paraguay, a starling's wing in France...

'There is something else that links all of these photographs,' Dr Ray said. 'Every plant, animal and human that features in these photographs came into being three years ago during the same twenty-one hour period.'

Dr Kumar shook her head in bemusement as she looked at more and more of the photographs, each of which showed a plant, animal or human with the exact same marking: an area of darker pigmentation in the form of a cluster of seven tiny shapes, each of which looked uncannily like a letter and together spelled the words:

'I am here.'

For longer stories by Mike Russell

please visit:

www.strangebooks.com

strange novels, novellas and short story collections

"Strange, surreal, odd, but absolutely immersive,
Mike Russell has created his own area of fiction."
Advocate Of Books
"Russell's stories are humorous, engaging and
poetically direct." *Beautiful Bizarre Magazine*
"Mike Russell seems to have mastered the art of
throwing absurdities onto paper, while keeping his
writing bright and interesting at the same time."
Cultured Vultures
"Beyond cool, well beyond ordinary, and just so
what I needed right now." *Oddly Weird Fiction
Reviews*

Inspiring, liberating, otherworldly, magical, surreal, bizarre, funny, disturbing, unique... all of these words have been used to describe the stories of Mike Russell so put on your top hat, open your third eye and enjoy... Nothing Is Strange!

"Nothing Is Strange is a unique collection of short stories that takes readers to bizarre places and lets them experience dreamlike situations that I have yet to read in other books." *Readers' Favorite*
"Funny, quirky, bizarre and thought-provoking." *The Contemporary Small Press*
"Full of stories of awareness, humour and wonder. I can't recommend this collection enough." *Readers Enjoy Authors Dreams*
"It is impossible to put it down before you finish it. A delight!!!" *Chasing Euphoria*
"This book is an experience!!!! Do I recommend it? Yes, a thousand yes." *Books & Travel Forever*

Nothing Is Strange by Mike Russell:
20 mind-expanding short stories

Does magic exist? Charlie Watson thinks it does and he wants to tell you all about it. Charlie tells of the strange events that led him from England to the Arctic, to perform the extraordinary feat that made him famous, and he finally reveals whether that extraordinary feat was magic or whether it was just a trick. (Suitable for adults of all ages.)

"Incredibly unique! I have genuinely never read anything like this before. I'm absolutely in love with this strange, magical book." *Into New Realms Reviews*
"Simply breath-taking." *Bunny's Pause Reviews*
"Magic is bursting with magical, wonderful things. I can't recommend this enough." *The Faerie Review*
"I think it would be difficult NOT to enjoy this book. I will be adding Mike Russell's other books to my 'to be read' list!" *This Brilliant Day*
"A fun book to get you through hard times. I hope you check it out as well as other works by the author. Russell is one of the best surrealist writers." *Geek Declassified*

Magic: a novel by Mike Russell

Printed in Great Britain
by Amazon